I Am the Best:
Princess Pam

I Am the Best:
Princess Pam

Maureen Nwajiobi

I AM THE BEST: PRINCESS PAM

iUniverse books may be ordered through booksellers or by contacting:

iUniverse
1663 Liberty Drive
Bloomington, IN 47403
www.iuniverse.com
844-349-9409

Because of the dynamic nature of the Internet, any web addresses or links contained in this book may have changed since publication and may no longer be valid. The views expressed in this work are solely those of the author and do not necessarily reflect the views of the publisher, and the publisher hereby disclaims any responsibility for them.

Any people depicted in stock imagery provided by Getty Images are models, and such images are being used for illustrative purposes only.
Certain stock imagery © Getty Images.

ISBN: 978-1-6632-3962-4 (sc)
ISBN: 978-1-6632-3963-1 (e)

Print information available on the last page.

iUniverse rev. date: 05/05/2022

To the Daughters of Mary
Mother of Mercy (DMMM)

To my family and in loving memory of my dear parents,
Mr. and Mrs. Michael Nwajiobi

Contents

Preface

This book is a fictional account using a palace setting to tell a story of high class and low-class individuals, a story about humiliation and oppression of the poor, especially poor workers, it is also a story that relates how to be nice to the poor, how to appreciate the poor regardless of their position in the society. The book portrays people living in a palace and the different characters they presented but the main message describes how arrogance and pride ruin individuals and society. The book displayed that love is reciprocal, that the amount that you give is related to what you will receive. If you hate, people will tend to hate you back. If you disrespect and look down on people around you, they will stay away from you, and you will be lonely and depressed.

Princess Pam, the main character, allowed her mother the queen to brainwash her into believing that she is the best and other low-class people are not important and she can disregard and disrespect them.

Her father, the king and the prince have different opinion, they encourage her to love and respect people regardless of their social status. Princess Pam chose to ignore the good advice of the king and adhered to the queen's advice which nearly ruined her life. Her friendship with a humble princess Amanda from a richer kingdom helped her to change. Fortunately, the queen also changed and started showing respect to all people after something unimaginable happened in the palace.

The major aim of the book is to prove that showing love and respect are better than racism, segregation, exclusion, discrimination, and arrogance. Princess Pam instead of showing love and respect she chose to disrespect people of a lower cast, and she became a sad and lonely person. On the other hand, the prince chose to obey his father, the king, he helped poor people and he even fell in love with a poor girl, and he is happy.

The author has experienced the effects of discrimination and how it was truly emotionally devastating, and heart breaking and encourages everyone to be kind and nice to people regardless of their social status.

I want to thank the members of my religious family, the Daughters of Mary Mother of Mercy for their encouragement and support. I wish to express my gratitude to Fr. Livinus Torty, MSP for his advice and support, and Fr. Martin J. Lott, OP for his valuable advice. I thank Mr. Tom Furmanczyk for editing the manuscript. I also thank the members of my natural family, the Nwajiobi family, especially my brother, Fr.

Michael Jude Nwajiobi, for his support. I also remember my late parents, Mr. Michael and Mrs. Catherine Nwajiobi,

Sr. Maureen Nwajiobi DMMM
Houston, Texas, November 2022

Introduction

Princess Pam is an arrogant princess; the queen formed her into believing that she is superior and more important than other people. She believes that other poor people are worthless in fact they treated house staff as if they are not humans. The people of the kingdom suffer much humiliation from her and her mother the queen. The king and the prince have a different value system even though people strongly believe that royals are superior to other citizens of their kingdom, they respect all people and treat them like human beings. The prince listened to his father's advice and example of life while the princess followed her mother's teaching and example that gave her the wrong orientation about life and society. The princess does not believe in humility, she believed her mother's high-class and low-class teaching. Her mother taught her that royals are in high class and other people are low class, especially poor people in the society. She was led to believe that arrogance and pride are virtues. The princess later had an encounter that changed the arc of her life.

Princess Pam who insisted that people call her the princess, visited princess Amanda who exemplified humility despite her high social status. Princess Amanda asked everyone to call her Amanda, she respects people and shows them love and kindness. When Princess Pam visited Amanda, her boring life of loneliness and hatred changed for good. She began to show love and received love in return. Everyone began to reciprocate and appreciate her newfound life. She discovered for herself that life can be boring and depressing when you cage yourself in arrogance and pride without regard for people around you. Her new life of love and happiness attracted princess Amanda's brother and they fell in love that later resulted in marriage.

Princess Pam regretted her previous attitudes and blamed her mother the queen for training her to treat people like worthless people. She realized that her father, the king, and the prince had been telling her the truth. She goes to them for guidance to make progress in her newfound life. Princess Pam's friendship with princess Amanda exposed her to new skills like learning how to cook. Her new life pleased everyone in the palace and beyond except for the queen, but when the queen realized that Princess Pam had profoundly changed, and she is no longer receptive to her high-low-class theory, the queen realized that she is alone, and her theories and opinion does no longer count or matter. The queen decided to change and started treating people with respect only after the unimaginable happened in the palace.

Chapter 1

Brain washed

Ringland is a small but beautiful town endowed with natural and beautiful surroundings. Tourists go to see the waterfall and lakes. The windy sway of tall green well-arranged trees is conducive to peaceful atmosphere. Ringland weather is just like spring, it is not too hot or too cold. The weather attracts visitors to the kingdom. The waterfall is indescribable, you cannot help but praise God for his wonderful creation. It is hard to see and find out where the water that continually runs comes from. It is beautifully shaped that people flock there to look at it and take pictures. When they post the pictures in the social media, more tourists flock the kingdom to witness the scene.

Schools take advantage of the waterfall. Teachers bring their students there to study the place, draw pictures and write poems, stories, or a composition about the waterfall. School children also visit the lake and many other beautiful places in the kingdom. The kingdom has a gigantic museum where they display their artefacts. They have archaeological anthropologists who oversee the Museum. The kingdom keeps and maintains all kinds of memorable sculptures, art works and pictures of former kings and their achievements in the kingdom. The anthropologists gather information from the neighboring kingdoms, and countries. This information built up an important and powerful source of information for the students in schools especially students studying arts, anthropology, geography, and history.

A king oversees the affairs of the kingdom and tries to develop the kingdom the much he can. All the people in the kingdom respect him and his family. They duly recognize him and his family as the reputable citizens of their kingdom. The king (Ife) has a wife (Ije), a son (George), the prince and a daughter (Pam), the princess. They have a group of domestic staff that take care of their needs. The house staff, gate keeper, and the cook discharge their duties to the royal family in the palace. The king pays them very well for their services.

Even though the people of the kingdom give effusive praise to the king and administration of the royal palace, the king and the prince regard the people of their kingdom with human respects. They do not to allow their position in high society affect them negatively. The queen of the kingdom, the king's wife and the daughter, the princess are arrogant and entitled. They disrespect people because of their lower social status.

The queen and the princess have shown their arrogance in many ways in the kingdom. According to the royal order, the prince and the princess should not go alone outside the palace for security reasons. The humble prince does not like the order because he feels suffocated, he wanted to be free. He once told his father, the king "Father, I want to ask you one favor, can I be allowed to go outside the palace alone?" The king told him that he already knew the answer to the question, which is, "No." The prince pleaded with the king but failed. Princess Pam loves the idea of going out with her house staff and the driver if she needs to go far. She abuses the opportunity given to her by ordering the house staff and the driver around. She threatens to tell her mother the queen to fire them if they misbehave. These maidens do not want to come around her or go anywhere with her because things can go wrong.

Princess Pam likes to stroll round the kingdom. One beautiful calm but breezy morning, she decided to stroll through the kingdom for fresh air. When she came out in her pink, brown beautiful royal regalia, she looked amazing like the sun rise. Her tall slim physique makes her look more beautiful in the royal outfit. The moment she mentioned that she would like to go for a stroll, two house staff are already waiting for her arrival in front of the palace building. They follow her standing at her back to accompany and protect her. The way the princess walks betrays her show of arrogance. She expects everyone to greet her first including the elders. Typically, younger people should respect their elders, the princess would not hear of it. She expects everyone to greet and acknowledge her as the princess. As she walks like a peacock, an elderly man passed by without greeting her.

The princess was furious for the elderly man's failure to greet her. She rained abuses on the man, "Are you a stranger in this land? Are you blind that you could not see me coming?" The man was so dumfounded that he could not find a word to express his embarrassment. Most of the people they met on their way greeted and accorded her the respect that she demanded. While she was still mad at the behavior of the man, an educated girl that knows her rights also passed without greeting her, the princess started her usual demand for respect. The girl looked at her with a surprised face and said, "Halloo, excuse me, are you referring to me?" The girl told the princess that she should mind her business. She further declared in her anger that she is disappointed with the princess for such display of arrogance in this twenty second century. The girl told her that no one is superior to the other and if the princess wants greetings, she should greet first, and the person she greets can choose to respond. She concluded, pointing at the princess, she said, "learn to respect other people and other people will reciprocate, stop terrorizing people with your pride."

Princess Pam was shocked at what happened, she rarely received such responses from the citizens of the kingdom. She was angry at the girl for insulting her in the presence of her house staff. The house staffs were surprised too but they were secretly happy for the way the girl responded to the princess. The princess made inquiries to find out who the girl was so that she might report her, and the queen will punish her. She was disappointed when she could not find the girl. Though she was frustrated at what the girl did, she knew that what the girl said was right. She ran to her mother the queen in frustration and recounted the story to her. She told the queen that she thinks the girl was most probably right when she said that we have equal rights, and no one person is superior to the other. The queen was terribly angry at the girl. She discouraged the princess from thinking about equality. She told her categorical that they are superior to other citizens and whoever goes against it will receive a severe punishment. She encouraged the princess to continue her entitled attitude.

Chapter 2

Arrogance is a disease

Princess Pam is naturally close to her mother, and she takes her advice seriously. After the encounter she had with the girl on the day she was strolling, she wanted to change her attitude having listened to what the girl said. However, the queen reassured her "You are a princess, you are not like them. You are superior to them, and they are nobody before you." The princess regained her composure after her mother's advice. She started insulting people both inside the palace and outside. The king is not happy with his daughter's rude behaviours. He cautioned his wife the queen to refrain from misleading their daughter. Prince George is the opposite of the princess. He respects people and he has many friends among them.

Fredrick, a fair robust boy visited the prince in the palace, and princess's attitude made him leave in tears before the prince could come out. It was the prince who invited him to the palace. He met Fredrick on his way home. The prince nearly hit Fredrick with his car when he tried to cross the road. He was angry with Fredrick for risking his life but when he realized that Fredrick has a lot going on in his mind, he decided to stop and asked what happened. Fredrick recounted his problems; he was running to buy a medication from a medicine store in their area. He focused his mind on getting the medication to save his mother's life, when the prince nearly hit him with his car. The prince invited him to the palace to help him with money.

"What is wrong with you princess? Why must you disrespect people with such hatred?" The prince roared at the princess. The princess ignored him and arrogantly walked like a peacock in front of him, making him angrier. The prince raised his hand, but he could not hit the princess. He ran into the palace and met his parents in the living room. He complained about princesses' attitude towards Fredrick, the poor boy. The king was not happy with what he heard. This was not the first time the princess insulted and humiliated people in his presence. The king angrily cautioned the princess to desist from her wicked attitude towards people. The queen did not see anything wrong with what the princess did. She told the king and the prince to stop harassing the princess for chasing away the dirty commoner from the palace.

The prince asked the guards on duty to take him to Fredrick's place. When he reached, Fredrick was talking with his mother. When Fredrick saw the prince, he stood up immediately and shouted, "The prince is here" "You came?" The prince did not respond, but went to him, embraced him, and apologized for the humiliation he encountered in the palace. The prince gave them a huge amount of money and promised to pay for Fredrick's mother's medication. He said to them "Do not bother yourself anymore. I will always help you." Fredrick jumped in excitement. His mother was so happy, she said, "My son, God bless you for your kindness and support." Prince stayed briefly with them and left. Before his departure, he gave Fredrick a telephone handset and advised him to communicate with him before visiting him at the palace to avoid a repeat of what happened.

When the prince returned to the palace, he met the princess on her way out for a walk. The princess said to the prince, "I know you have gone to see that impoverished dirty boy" she said as she gloriously walked like a peacock towards the prince. She kept saying that she could not understand why her brother the prince behaves like a commoner. "I don't know why you refuse to understand that there is a huge social distance between royalty and poor rotten commoners, brother" thundered the princess at the prince. The prince walked up to her and drew her close to him and warned her sternly. He told her that she is supposed to have human heart. "You should be nice to people; you should show them love and not maltreat them" He pushed her slightly and left her. The princess almost fell on the ground. She managed to hold herself. One of the house staff quickly ran to her to ascertain that she was all right. She slapped her so hard that the housekeeper fell to the ground. She ordered all the house staff and guards around there to go away. She was still angry at what the prince did in the presence of the workers.

The prince made up his mind to help Fredrick and his family. He told the king about his visit to Fredrick's family and what he discovered. He told the king that it will be nice to help the family because of their poverty. He explained how Fredrick's mother had been sick for a long time and they have no money for her medication. He explained how Fredrick could not go to school despite his intelligence. The king agreed with the prince that it is important to assist the family. He told the prince to send Fredrick's mother to a good hospital where they could take care of her and treat her illness. He also told the prince that they will sponsor Fredrick to the highest level of education. "Yes, thank you Dad" The prince shouted with excitement. He hurriedly rushed back to Fredrick's house to deliver the good news and send Fredrick's mother to a good hospital. Before he left, the king told him to go to his bedroom and bring his bag. The king gave the prince some money to give to Fredrick's family.

Fredrick and his mother were overjoyed at the news. As they were still joyous, Angel, Fredrick's senior sister came back from the market and greeted the prince. She curiously wanted to know the reason there was jubilation. When they told her what happened, she thanked the prince and danced with her family. The prince liked Angel the moment he set his eyes on her. He admired her and kept his thoughts to himself. He sent Fredrick's mother to a renowned hospital, where they treated her properly. The prince gave them the money and went back to the palace. Fredrick, Angel, and their mother were so excited at the kind treatment from the king and his son. They thanked God for answering their prayers. They wondered why the queen and the princess were so different from the king and the prince. Fredrick looked at his sister intently and spoke. "He liked you" "who" responded Angel. "The prince of course, didn't you notice how he looked at you," Fredrick said smiling at Angel. Angel giggled and with a wave of hand dismissed him.

Chapter 3

Why are they like this?

Fredrick's family planned to visit the palace to thank the king and his family. The day they visited, they took some fruits and vegetables and a gift for the king and the prince. When they arrived, the gate keeper refused to open the gate for them. Fredrick had earlier called the prince but could not reach him. When they were arguing with the gate keeper, the princess came out "who are the idiots disrupting the peace of this palace," she shouted, walking majestically to the gate. The gate keeper heard her voice and started shivering. He stammered when he was trying to describe the situation. When she went close to the gate, he saw Fredrick and shouted, "You again, what are you doing here?" Fredrick introduced his mother and pointing at their gifts, he wanted to explain to the princess that they came to thank the king. The princess could not allow him to finish before she commanded them to leave the palace with their worthless gifts. They pleaded with her to allow them to see the king and the prince, but she refused. She instructed the gate keeper to close the gate.

Fredrick and his mother sorrowfully left the palace. They were still on their way to their house when they met the prince driving home in his car. He stopped and asked them where they were coming from. They explained what happened and the prince was mad at the princess. He apologized for not answering Fredrick's call. He explained that they have been in a crucial meeting in their company. He told them to enter his car so that he can take them back to the palace, but they refused. They would rather give him the gifts than encountering the princess again. When the prince insisted, they decided to enter the car. They followed him to the palace. When they came out of the car, the princess was furious at the prince. The prince did not utter a word to the princess. He took Fredrick and his mother by the hand and went into the palace to see the king.

The king was happy to receive them. He told the house staff to serve them food and drink. They ate and were satisfied. The king also gave them some food stuffs. He told the house staff to receive and keep the fruits and vegetables they brought to him. While they were chatting with the king and the prince, the queen came into the large well decorated living room where they were. Fredrick and his mother greeted her; she mumbled a response to them with a wave of hand. She could not understand why the king received these poor wretched people in their living room. She believed that such people should stay far away because they are like animals, and they are not supposed to come close to the palace or inside the living room. She was angry with them, the king and the prince who received them and sat comfortably with them regardless of their status.

The queen stepped outside the living room and found the princess fuming and panting up and down in anger. They shared the same opinion about how Fredrick and his mother smell of poverty and how such people belong to their cage as animals. As they were still talking, the prince came out with Fredrick and his mother. They were frightened when they saw the princess and the queen. The prince ignored them and told Fredrick and his mother to enter his car so that he can take them back to their house. "Why must you take them in your car, can't they walk? Why are you always coming here? Stay in your home, we do not want you here" screamed the princess at Fredrick and his mother. Fredrick was angry at what the princess said. He felt bad because the princess insulted his mother. He could not utter a word. The queen called the prince and told him to see her inside the house. The prince refused; he told the queen that he will answer when he comes back. He immediately drove out with Fredrick and his mother.

The princess was frustrated because of what the prince did. She requested a cup of water, and the housekeeper brought the water with a trembling hand for fear of the princess. Tiny drops of water landed on princesses' foot, and she took the water and poured it on the housekeeper in anger. When the housekeeper cried out in discomfort because the water was cold, the princess called her back and slapped her so hard that she nearly fell on the ground. The prince entered in, and he witnessed the action of the princess. He walked to the princess and screamed "Why are you behaving like a beast? We are supposed to protect our people and not to kill or subject them to torture. You need to stop, stop, this is wickedness." The princess was very angry because the prince insulted her in the presence of the workers. She hurriedly followed the prince inside the living room, screaming his name. She ran to their mother the queen and complained about the prince. The queen expressed her frustration against the prince. She reassured her daughter that there is a huge demarcation between them and other people. They should remain in their position. "I do not understand why it is difficult for the prince to understand" The queen stammered in anger.

The princess went to her room wondering the reason behind prince's behaviour towards those poor people. She wondered why such people are so dirty and poor. She wondered why they beg for money all the time thereby disrupting the peace in the palace. "I hate them,

I hate them with a passion" The princess expressed in rage. She suddenly stood up from her bed and started pacing up and down. She planned her strategy which is to deal with the poor people that will visit the palace and to mercilessly punish the palace workers when they misbehave. She strongly believed that her behaviour is the only way to gain respect from these commoners. She thought that intimidating them and terrorizing them would put fear in them thereby demonstrating her supremacy.

Chapter 4

I am lonely

As time goes by the princess realizes that instead of gaining respect from people, they hate and despise her. Every one of them loved the prince. She wondered why it is like that. The prince does not punish them. He loved and respected them. He does not show superiority over them, yet they accord him huge respect and love. She realized that the prince has many friends. Some of them come to visit him at the palace and he visits them. The prince is free with the palace staff, he treats them like friends, and they love him dearly. She noticed that the prince is incredibly happy and content while she is not. She does not have friends and she is lonely and unhappy. Though she craves for power and authority, she is human, and desires love and attention.

An incident that surprised her and made her think was when the prince visited a friend for one week. When he came back to the palace, the workers celebrated as if their messiah came back. They were so happy that they ignored the princess when she ordered them to stop making noise in the palace. They missed the prince, and they were happy to see him. Shortly after the incident she visited her cousin for a change of environment and avoids her loneliness and frustration. When she returned after a few days, the palace workers were not particularly happy to see her return. Some of them ran away on seeing her. She overheard some of them gossiping and hissing. She could not punish them because the incident crumbled her emotion. She felt sad and rejected.

When she complained to her mother, the queen comforted and told her that she should ignore them and when any of the palace staffs misbehaves, they should receive severe punishment. She told her that she is a princess, and she should carry herself like a princess. Whenever the princess wants to repent from her evil deeds, the queen will always encourage her to continue to belittle people. The princess was closer to the queen than the king. She does not take the kings advice. She prefers to trust her mother's judgement and advice. Her only devoted friend is her mother, and she learned a lot from her. She decided to continue to follow in her mother's footsteps despite her depression and loneliness. Her school friends deserted her because of her pride and sense of entitlement.

The king called the prince and reminded him that it is time to get a wife. He told the king that he should not worry because he has someone that he wants to marry. The king was surprised to hear that because he has not seen the prince with any girl. He persuaded him to bring the girl to the palace. They scheduled the day that he will bring his friend. In the morning of the day, he was supposed to present his prospective bride to the king; he went to Fredrick's place. He told Angel to accompany him somewhere. Angel's family trusted the prince, so Angel followed him. He took Angel for shopping. He bought a lot of beautiful clothes for her. She instructed Angel to change into some of the clothes they bought. They went to saloon and fixed her hair. Angel looked beautiful in her hair and outfit. He pleaded with her to escort him to the palace.

On reaching the palace, the prince held Angel's hand and walked inside the living room in the palace. He introduced the king to Angel and introduced Angel to the king. He went and called the queen and said 'Mother, here is the queen of my heart, she is the girl I intend to marry" Angel was shocked. She could not believe what she heard. She gave a surprised look to the prince "marry me? Are you serious?" The king laughed in confusion. "She didn't know that you intend to marry her?" The king asked the prince who kneeled before Angel and brought out a beautiful gold ring. Before the prince could open his mouth to propose to Angel, the queen screamed in anger, "stop it, who is she? Who is her father and mother, are they royalty?" Instead of answering the queen's numerous questions, the prince explained looking at the king "Father, I am sorry for doing it this way, I wanted to surprise her, and I love her so much and intend to spend the rest of my life with her"

The king looked at the prince and said, "I can see you love her; I trust your judgement, you have my blessing, but it will be important to make inquiries before the commencement of the marriage rites." "Thank you, dad," said the prince. Looking at the queen, "Please do not do this mother, I love this girl and I will need your blessing too" The prince stuttered at the queen who was already leaving the living room angrily. The queen told him that he can only give her blessing after the inquiries to avoid getting a poor gold digger as a wife. She left the room without looking back. The prince still kneeling asked Angel "Will you marry me?" Angel kneeled by his side, smiled at him, and said, "When you do not know who we are, you loved and cared for us, you defied all odds to associate with poor people like us, of course, I will marry you" She stretched out her fingers and displayed it in front of the prince. The prince happily slipped the ring in her finger. They embraced each other.

The prince told the king that Angel is Fredrick's older sister. He fell in love with her the first time he met her in their house. The king had no problem with their marriage. What about the queen and the princess?

When they realized who Angel was, they were mad at the prince. They stated categorically that it will never happen. They expressed that Angel, and her family are poor gold diggers trying to reap where they did not sow. The queen told the prince that the wretched family has charmed him. She explained that there are many beautiful young girls from rich, royal, and reputable homes where he can find a wife. When the prince ignored them, they swore to disrupt the marriage plans. Angel visited the prince in the palace one evening and while waiting for him, the princess walked towards her and rained abuses on her. She told her that she is a gold digger, and she can never marry the prince. Angel did not respond to her insults.

Angel kept mute and patiently waited for the prince. When he came out, they embraced and started playing around. This action infuriated the princess. They ignored her, while holding their hands, they laughed so hard that the princess started crying. She ran inside her room. She realized how lonely she has been. The prince is happy with her newfound love and fiancée, and she arrogantly chased away all those that attempted to love her. She cried so hard in her room. One of the maidens unfortunately came in at that moment to tell her that she had served lunch. She screamed at her and threatened to slap her. "Go away, you idiot" She cried. The princess realized that the more she wants to fight the prince and Angel the more depressed she became. "They seemed to be in love" she thought aloud. She started crying again. "When will I be in love like that"? She cried aloud "When you stop hating and start loving," said the prince. The princess felt ashamed when she realized that the prince heard what she said.

The prince sat down in her room and started advising her. He told her to stop hating people and show some love. 'When you love people, people love you in return, when you hate them, they will hate you, if you disregard and disrespect them, then they will disregard you." He told the princess that she is lonely and sad because she is proud, and she arrogantly refuses to show love to people including her friends. He told her that it is not too late, she can start loving and she will see the difference. The princess kept quiet and when she did not respond to him, he left her room. When the prince left the room, the princess wanted him to stay and continue to talk but she could not tell him. She knew that the prince was speaking the truth, but she did not know how to help herself. She wanted to change but the support of the queen, her ego and pride will not allow her to change.

The king called the whole family and informed them that the prince will go ahead and marry Angel since they found nothing that will hinder the marriage according to their tradition. Angel and the prince later got married. The queen and the princess tried to frustrate Angel, but she always ignored their attitude. When the princess was tired of fighting someone who does not fight back, she gave up. The princess started respecting Angel the day she overheard what Angel told her friend that came to visit her. Angel's friend visited her and wanted to know how Angel was coping with the princess regarding her pride. Angel replied and said pleasant things about the princess. The princess overheard that, and she changed her mind and started liking Angel.

Chapter 5

Life is boring

One hot afternoon, the princess went to the palace garden to get fresh air. She was trying to settle down and start reading a novel when a car pulled inside the palace. The king of the neighboring kingdom showed up with his daughter. The princess looked up to find out who came to their palace. She looked and recognized the girl that came into their palace with a man. She knew that she had met that face, but she was not sure where she met him. She went to meet them and realized that the girl was the girl she met during her University days. She ran up to her in excitement and the girl recognized her immediately and screamed "princess." They hugged each other. The princess looked at her and noticed that she dressed like a princess. She asked her "Are you a princess?" The girl laughed and nodded in affirmation.

The princess was surprised because the girl never showed during the University days that she was a princess.

The girl's name is Amanda, a princess from the neighboring kingdom. She prefers everyone to call her Amanda and not princess. She is the only daughter of King Henry. She came with her father to see the king, princess's father regarding the upcoming celebration in their kingdom. The princess felt so bad that she has been making a fool of herself. She felt stupid that when they were studying in the university, she was so proud, telling everyone that she is a princess while Amanda, a princess from such wealthy kingdom was so humble and did not even tell anyone on campus that she was a princess. She was surprised to see the way Amanda responded to the greeting from the house staff. Amanda greeted them with regard and respect. The princess was ashamed when she realized how happy and humble Amanda was in school.

The princess remembered how arrogant she was in school; she used to brag and tell anyone that cared to listen that they are rich and royalty. But look at Princess Amanda, she is a princess and never mentioned it to anyone and her father is richer than her father, but she never bragged about it.

The princess exchanged contact information with Amanda. Princess promised Amanda that she will visit her sometime. The princess was excited to meet an old school mate. She decided that she will keep her as a friend. After some weeks, when she needed a vacation, she called Amanda and told her that she would like to visit her and stay for the weekend. "Oh cool, we will be glad to have you around" said Amanda to the princess. When she was leaving, the workers in the palace were incredibly happy. They wanted her to stay wherever she was going for a long time, at least there will be peace in the palace. When she arrived in Amanda's palace, they received her warmly. She was happy for a change of scene and to reduce her worries.

The house staffs in Amanda's palace served food, fruits, and drinks. The princess got mad at one of the house staffs who tried to ask her how smooth her journey was. "How is that your business? Learn to mind your business" Amanda was not happy with such response and attitude coming from the princess. Amanda was not so surprised because she knew the princess to be a proud and arrogant person. She confronted her immediately and advised her to quit being rude to people. "The girl is trying to show concern and love." As Amanda was still talking, the housekeeper that was serving became tensed because of the way their visitor responded to her greeting, she bumped on the princess's leg and some drops of water dropped on her lap. The princess stood up in a flash and wanted to slap her, but Amanda stood up and held her hand just on time.

Amanda told the housekeeper to leave. She looked at the princess for a long time and said, "Are you this mean? "To be honest with you, I do not keep friends that are mean to other people or their workers, these people are human beings." The princess remembered what her brother the prince told her recently, she was sorry for her deeds. She does not want to lose Amanda's friendship. She apologized to her and promised to be nicer to people. She wanted to say that the food is not good to discredit the cook that prepared the food but remembered what princess Amanda said and said "wow… it tastes good" Instead. Amanda smiled at her and said, "Thank you." The princess wanted to know why she thanked her, and she explained that she prepared the food. Surprised the princess said "You prepared the food? How do you mean? You cook?" Princess Amanda explained to her that she likes to cook. She learned how to prepare a lot of food from her mother the queen.

The princess was surprised because she does not know how to boil water. One of the house staff in her palace does the cooking, they wash her clothes and even make her bed. She does not know how to do a lot of things. She thought about her mother, the queen of their kingdom spoiled her. She resolved to change from her evil antisocial ways and start being nice to people. She asked Amanda to teach her how to cook. Amanda promised to teach her all she needs to know. She was happy for visiting Amanda. The visit had changed her life. She learned that it pays to be humble and nice. She realized that she is happier now that she has started loving and showing respect to people. She noticed that the house staff felt more relaxed with her, and they show her love in return. She realized that life was too boring and lonely when she was mean and disrespectful to people. She learned how to prepare a lot of food from Amanda.

The princess enjoyed her visit. She called her parents and informed them that she will not come home as she planned, she will stay for few more days. One of the house staff overheard the discussion, and informed other servants that the princess will return later. They were happy to hear the good news. They felt that God answered their prayers because they have been praying for her to stay longer.

The princess had made lots of new friends before leaving Amanda's palace. She called the house staff and other workers in the palace and gave them parting gifts before returning to her kingdom. The workers and the house staff received their gifts with thanks. They were really amazed at the transformation of the princess considering her superior attitude when she first arrived in their palace. They hugged her and bade her goodbye.

Amanda accompanied the princess back to her palace. She promised the princess that she will surely visit her soon. The two princesses planned to go for site seeing trip. They planned and fixed a date when they are to visit and spend quality time in the most beautiful tourist places in their respective kingdoms.

Chapter 6

My soul is at peace

When the princess returned home. She has changed tremendously. She is now humble, respectful, and nice to people. More importantly she has learned how to cook delicious meals. Amanda escorted the princess to her palace and left. The house staff in front of the palace when she arrived came and welcomed her with concerned faces. She smiled at them and thanked them for getting her bag. The house staff were still trying to find out if they heard right, she asked them how they were doing. Surprised, the house staff reluctantly answered that they are doing well still unsure if she meant it or not. She greeted and acknowledged all the workers she met on her way inside the palace. They were all amazed at princess's sudden change of behavior.

The king and some of his cabinet members were at the sitting room when she entered. The king noticed her change of attitude immediately as she entered the room because of her smile and the way she greeted everyone in the room. She used to ignore the cabinet members regarding them as dirty low-class gold diggers and beggars. She does no longer regard humans as animals. Her attitude surprised and pleased the king. The queen and the prince were happy to welcome her back to the palace. Angel, prince's wife was amazed at the princess when she saw her and hugged her with joy. Angel was somehow suspicious of the change initially but when the princess apologized to her for her superior attitude towards her, she was happy.

For the first time the princess noticed that Angel was pregnant, she remarked "Girl, are you pregnant?" Angel smiled and nodded in confirmation. 'Oh, my goodness, I did not notice because I was too arrogant to notice you or your pregnancy" the princess screamed. She held Angel and said, "Can you ever forgive me for being mean to you ever since you stepped into this palace, I am truly sorry, please forgive me." They hugged each other and Angel told her that she has nothing against her, and she has forgiven her. The king and the prince were overjoyed when they saw the princess and Angel holding hands and laughing together. They thanked God for princess's new lifestyle. The queen was surprised and irritated at the new character that the princess was showing. She was anxious to know what happened. The princess explained in the presence of everyone that she regretted her previous attitude. She apologized to everyone and promised to continue to be nicer and respectful.

The princess stated that she learnt a lot from her friend, Princess Amanda who happens to be her school mate when they were at the university. She felt ashamed of herself that Amanda was very humble and nice to people without showing off like she did despite that she is a princess from a powerful kingdom. The princess later brought out some goodies she bought for the house staff and workers in the palace. They were surprised at her kindness. They knew instantly that this was a way of apologizing to them. They were pleased at her new behavior. They all have peace of mind. It is only the queen that is out of place in the palace with her arrogance and the low-class theory. She views house staff, other domestic workers and other people that are not royalty as low-class. The princess learned it from her, but the princess has changed.

The princess now socializes and mingles with everyone in the palace. The most surprising event was that the princess dismissed the cook from the kitchen and prepared a delicious meal. They were all amazed at her total transformation. They enjoyed the meal, and the king was proud of her. He told her to keep up the good work that she is doing. The princess blamed her mother, the queen for her past misbehavior. She explained that the queen raised her to be proud and arrogant.

The princess praised the king for his kindness. She acknowledged that the King has been encouraging her to be humble and regard people as humans and not as animals. She regretted disobeying her father. She wondered why it took her so long to realize how mean her behavior had been. She regretted hurting a lot of people. She made up her mind to continue to be nice and kind to people disregarding their social status.

The princess realized that she is happier now than before. She realized that despite her royal status she was still sad and lonely because she refused to show love, she was arrogant and refused to show respect to other people. She realized that love and respect is reciprocal. Since she learned a lot from the king, she goes closer and closer to the king, the prince, and his wife Angel. She used to be extremely close to the queen but not any longer. She avoids speaking or staying with the queen for fear of her wrong indoctrinations. When the queen realized that the princess has changed totally and she is not ready to agree with her anymore, she realized that she is isolated in her arrogance and low-class theory, and she slowed down. Peace and happiness reigned in the palace. The domestic workers are no longer stressed and sad, they are happy.

The princess was happy with her friendship with Amanda. She has learned a lot from her. Their relationship suddenly got the attention of Amanda's brother, the prince. He fell in love with the princess, and they started dating. The princess reflected on her life and thanked God for what she had become. She realized that Amanda's brother took notice of her because she has changed. He could not have noticed her when she was arrogant and mean to people. She thanked Amanda for coming into her life. She was grateful for her total transformation and happiness.

Chapter 7

Unimaginable

The princess kept her decision to be nice and humble. She greeted her elders without waiting for them to greet her. She does not order the house staff around. She is happier with herself. She compared her life of arrogance, hatred, disrespect, loneliness, and misery and her new life of humility, love, respect, friendship, and happiness and realized that respect and love are reciprocal. She noticed that she caged herself with hatred for other people and she nearly died of depression and hatred. She imagined the reason behind the decision of the queen to have such hatred for the poor people. She thanked God for rescuing her from her mother's oppressive footsteps.

The friendship between the princess and Amanda's brother intensified. He proposed marriage to the princess, and she accepted. They invited many people to their engagement party. They were eating, drinking, and dancing. The princess was so happy that she danced so well, then suddenly she fainted and fell on the ground. They rushed her to the hospital where the doctor ran some tests to ascertain her problem. When the test result came out, Amanda's brother and the princess's family were surprised and shocked to learn that the princess had kidney failure. When the princess heard about the kidney failure, she cried so hard and pleaded for help because she did not want to die.

The princess's household, the king and the queen, the prince and his wife Angel, Amanda and her brother the princess's fiancée were all worried in the hospital when the doctor informed them that their hospital did not have a matching kidney for the princess. Even the kidneys of the two princes that offered to help did not match. Amanda even offered to donate her kidney, but it did not match. The doctor said that they will continue to look for a kidney that will match her kidney and if they cannot find any, another option is to send the princess abroad.

One of the house staff, her name is Elena whom the princess had previously maltreated and slapped lost her mother and she went home for the funeral. After the funeral she came back to the palace and resumed her duties. She heard everything that happened. How the princess has changed and become a nice person. She also heard about her deteriorating medical condition. She felt sorry for the princess. While she was still talking with the housekeeper that told her the story, the queen screamed on the phone. They ran to find out the reason she screamed, she fell on the ground and started crying, She kept saying that her only daughter cannot die. Realizing the reason she screamed, they consoled her and went back to their duty post.

That night Elena the housekeeper could not sleep. She kept pondering on the sickness of the princess. Even though the princess slapped her unnecessarily and maltreated her several times, she prayed for her healing. Early in the morning, she went to the queen and said, "I would like to go to the hospital and check if my kidney will match, I want to donate my kidney to her, if my poor kidney is worthy." The queen thought that Elena was sarcastic and looked at her in anger but looking at her face and realizing that she was sincere, she melted in tears and remembered how she had treated her like a useless person, how she had rained most humiliating verbal abuses on her. The queen asked for her forgiveness and thanked her for her good heart and generosity. She told Elena that even if her kidney did not match, she will still appreciate her good intentions to help her dying daughter.

Few minutes later, the queen and Elena went to the hospital to check if her kidney will match. On reaching the hospital, Elena went to see the doctor. While the queen was pacing up and down the hospital praying and hoping that Elena's kidney will match, two nurses hurriedly went to the princess's room and took her to the surgical room. The nurses were in such a hurry that they did not answer the queen. As the queen was still wondering what was going on, the king came with Angel and her husband the prince. After a few minutes, Amanda came with her brother the prince. They inquired what happened when they could not find the princess in her room. The queen told them what happened. While still talking, one of the nurses came out from the surgical room and told them that Elena's kidney matched, and the surgery went well.

The nurse informed them that they cannot see the princess and Elena until they wake up from anaesthesia and become conscious. They were surprised and at the same time happy that the princess will live. It was terribly hard to find a matching kidney. Realizing that the hospital finally found donated kidney. It was shocking because someone the princess earlier destroyed her image and reputation was the same person that saved her life.

They danced with so much joy that they forgot that they are in the hospital. The queen kept dancing and praising God. The king looked at her, called her by his side and reminded her that same girl, she humiliated and oppressed was the one that saved their daughter from dying. The king told her to learn her lessons and stop looking down on people because of their social status, he also reminded her that all humans are God's creatures, and we are all important. The queen told the king that she had repented and pleaded for Elena's forgiveness the moment she agreed to donate her kidney to her daughter.

The hospital later discharged the princess and Elena from the hospital. The king summoned the people of the kingdom to gather and celebrate and thank God for the healing of their daughter. He promoted Elena and raised her salary. He told her not to work as a house keeper in the palace; they made her a member of their royal family.

The good news was that the potentially tragic experience changed the queen, she started treating everyone as human and important. She started showing love and respect to all the workers in the palace. She even extended love, respect, and generosity to the whole kingdom. She called on poor women in the kingdom and gave them money to start businesses that will help sustain their family. She placed many orphan children on scholarship. She realized that she felt so happy doing good things than when she was doing selfish and dreadful things.

The king during one of their celebrations in the kingdom made it as a rule that anyone that verbally or physically destroys the image or reputation of another in the kingdom will receive punishment. The king made it clear that the whole kingdom should learn how to stop discrimination, segregation, humiliation. He told them that he wanted love and peace to overcome hatred in their kingdom. He concluded that human beings are important to each other, that human beings have their peculiar talent, and they need each other to work together and succeed. He proclaimed that they should not wait for those they oppress to save them before they learn to love and respect each other. When he said that part, the queen bowed down in penitence.

The two kingdoms held a remarkable and luxurious wedding celebration for Princess Pam and the prince from the other kingdom, Amanda's brother. It was a huge celebration filled with love and mutual understanding and respect for everyone. After the wedding, the princess packed all her belongings and moved to the other kingdom where she later became their queen. She reigned with her husband peacefully having learned how to lead people and treat them with respect. Amanda also got married to a prince charming from another kingdom. Their friendship continued. They continued to support and advice each other.

In conclusion

In this book, the author inspired by the destructive woes of discrimination, segregation, and racism in the society wrote a book that featured great lessons of acknowledging that humility is a virtue and arrogance is a disease, that humans are all important and no one is more important than anybody else. Using the palace as a setting for portraying what happens in the society. Princess Pam's character showed that it is not good to disregard or disrespect people, the lesson awakens in us the reality to learn that it is important to be nice to people regardless of their poor status. More importantly, nobody knows what will happen tomorrow, the poor person might save us or help us in life.

The princess was arrogant and rude, she treated people with hatred and disrespect and people hated her and her arrogance. She felt so lonely and unloved. When she met another princess that was even richer than her, she realized that the princess, who was humble, respectful, and lovely, in turn received much love and respect from all people.

The princess thought about her life and how miserable she was in spite of her royal status and riches; she was not happy. She repented after seeing the example of her good friend and the people that she offended forgave her. She also learned many good new skills like cooking for others. She decided to grow closer to the King, her father who had advised her to be kind and humble. She stayed away from the queen, her mother's toxic advice. When the queen realized that she is on her own with the low status mentality she moderated her input, and people were happy. However, something unimaginable happened in the palace which changed the perspective of the queen about the true value of poor people. The incident touched her life so profoundly, that she had an epiphany and started helping poor people instead of despising them. She started associating with people regardless of their social status.

Another key message in the book is that it is also important to keep good friends that will help us get better and not a friend that will lead us on the wrong path. Good friends are a treasure from God that we should cherish. In our society today many people tend to follow bad friends just to belong and to get along often times resulting in bad outcomes. Good and loyal friends help people to grow in good values and become more human.

The king and the prince exemplified a good example of humility and how we should communicate with each other, showing love and respect to people regardless of their position in the society. The queen portrayed the evil of racism and discrimination in society. It is important to respect and show love to everyone because when people show love, they receive love, when they show hatred to people, they often reciprocate with hatred.

The character of Angel in the book portrayed another significant virtue that people can use to teach the arrogant and mean people. Angel ignored the unruly behavior of the princess and did not say bad things against her, and that singular act contributed to the princess's attitude adjustment for the better.

Printed in the United States
by Baker & Taylor Publisher Services